# Time for Bed, the Babysitter Said

## Peggy Perry Anderson

 sandpiper

Green Light Readers

Houghton Mifflin Harcourt

Boston   New York

The Library of Congress has cataloged the hardcover edition as follows:
Anderson, Peggy Perry.
"Time for bed," the babysitter said.
Summary: Not even his babysitter's most strenuous efforts can convince
Joe the frog to go to bed.
[1. Frogs—Fiction. 2. Bedtime—Fiction. 3. Babysitters—Fiction.] I. Title.
PZ7.A54874Ti   1987   [E]   86-27388

ISBN: 978-0-395-41851-2 hardcover
ISBN: 978-0-547-85061-0 paperback

Manufactured in Mexico
RDT 10 9 8 7 6 5 4 3 2

4500385631

To my dad, Buzz Perry, who always said, "Maybe someday you'll draw pictures for kids' books."

"Time for bed,"
the babysitter said.

"No," said Joe.

"I said, time for bed."

And Joe said, "No."

"Come, come, you sleepyhead,
it is time to go to bed."

"No!"

"No!"

"No!"

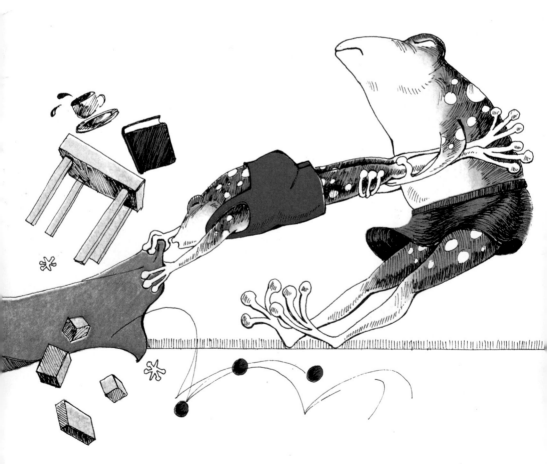

"No! No!"

"Let go."

"Get off," I said.

"Get off. Get off and go to bed."

"Get off! Get off! Get off my head!"

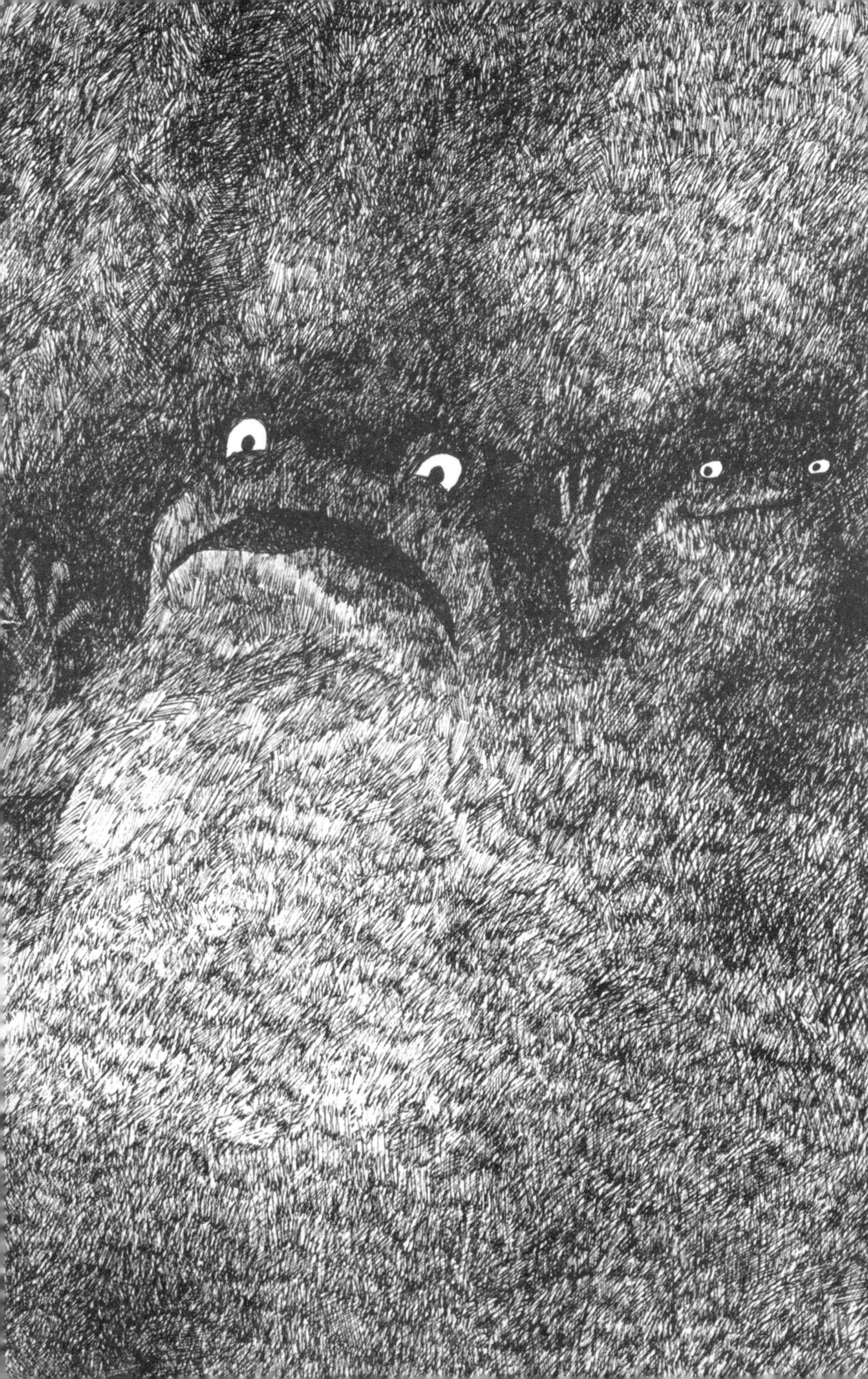

Click!

"Oh, no! Come back here, Joe!"

"Come out! Come out,
wherever you are!"

"I see you in that cookie jar!"

"Time for bed,"
the babysitter said.

"No," said Joe.

"No! No!"

"Joe, Joe," the babysitter said,
"why, oh why won't you go to bed?"

"Because you didn't say please," Joe said.

"Please, Joe, please go to bed."

And Joe did.

"You forgot to say thank you."